Fear the Bunny

Richard T. Morris and Priscilla Burris

A CAITLYN DLOUHY BOOK

 Atheneum Books for Young Readers • New York London Toronto Sydney New Delhi

Bunnies, bunnies, burning bright,

in the forests of the night—

Excuse me.

That's **not** how it goes.

It's "tiger, tiger, burning bright, in the forests of the night."

Here,
it's
"bunnies,
bunnies."

That's
ridiculous.

The poem is about . . .

ME!
The most
feared
animal
in the forest.

There's nothing scary
about a bunny.

In this forest, we fear the bunnies.

Fear

That's a good one!

the bunny.

Please run away.
Save yourself.

Look, I don't run away from anything, okay?

Have you seen these teeth? These claws?

Oooh, the **bunnies** are approaching.

Quick, someone check my vegetable garden.

You are in grave danger.
Hide now, before it's too late.

I can still see your tail.

That's it?
You've got to be kidding me.
A cotton ball
is more frightening
than that thing.
What's he going to do?
CUTE me to death?

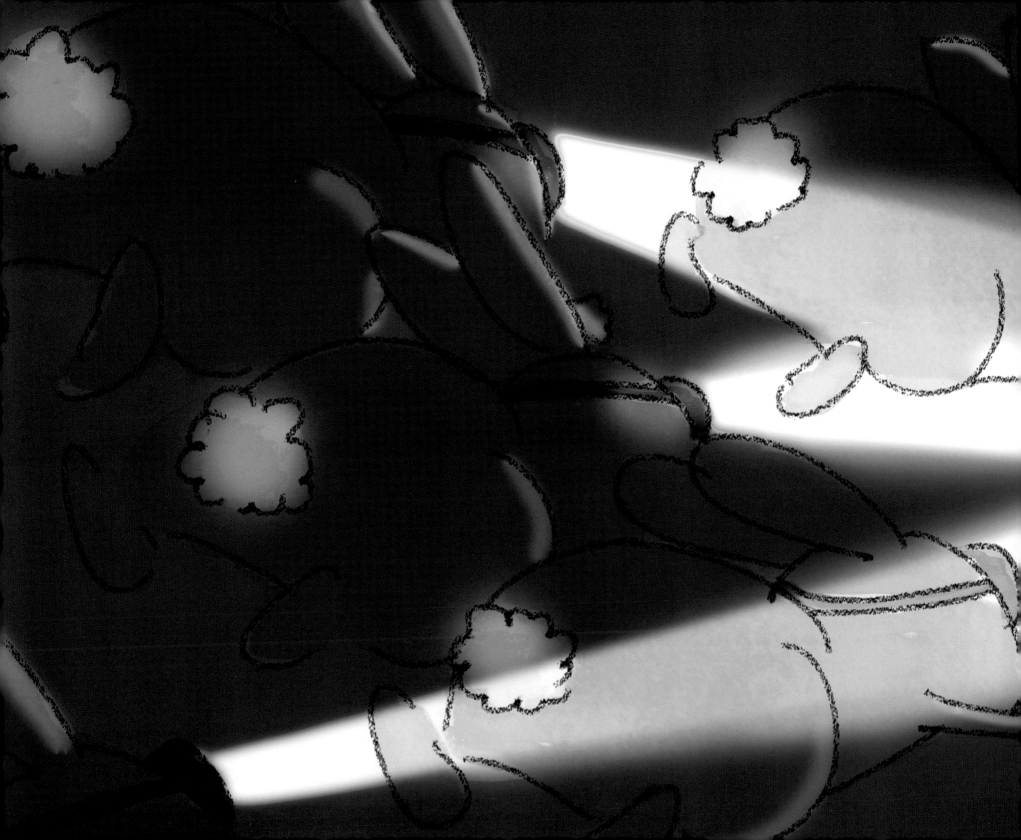

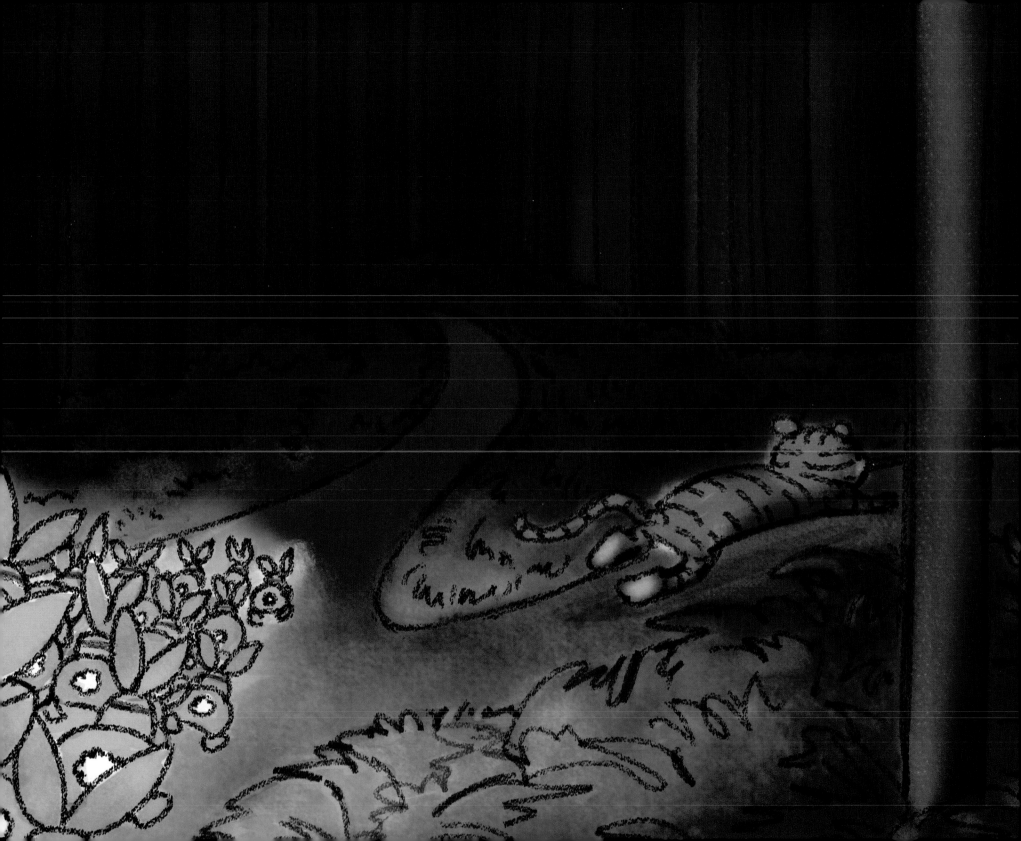

Bunnies, bunnies,

burning bright . . .

Bunnies, bunnies

~~Tyger Tyger,~~ burning bright,
In the forests of the night;
What immortal hand or eye,
Could frame thy fearful symmetry?

In what distant deeps or skies,
Burnt the fire of thine eyes?
On what wings dare he aspire?
What the hand, d...